You are Dearly Loved

Alice Opoku

ISBN: 9798845970466

This is a work of fiction. Any resemblance to actual events or persons, living or dead, is entirely coincidental.

Published by BKC Consulting(BKCink)
info@bkc.name

| +233244961121 | www.BKC. name

Contact the Author
Emai: alicebusybee@gmail.com
Tel: +1(248)675-5978

Dedication

To all the families affected by this tragedy, to those who shared their pain and void with me, and to all going through anything, they feel they can't tell anyone:

There is always HOPE, there is always a shoulder to lean and cry on, there is always someone around to listen. No situation is hopeless. Have FAITH.

Acknowledgements

Nana Teasebour Adwinasa-Poku

Nkabomhene in Nkwantakese, in the Ashante Region of Ghana.

A man who has seen the rise in teenage pressures that have led many to commit suicide and decided to fund this project. Nana thank you.

Contents

Introduction

"Hang in there" they always say, but hanging in can be tough, draining and heart-wrenching.

No matter how hard you try, you are bound to encounter tough situations, you are bound to make mistakes, do things or meet people you regret ever meeting. With the pressure from social media and the fast life on the rise, teenagers are always trying to catch up. Nobody wants to go through the traditional and slow way of making wealth and riches, everyone now wants to build bigger houses, ride the fastest cars and have the most beautiful things without working for them.

...and when they are being left behind, they have to run and catch up.

Life can be hard and rough at times but suicide is never an option. Yes, it sometimes gets darker and darker just like a rabbit hole with no end in sight. Don't choose it. There is always light at the end of the tunnel.

Hang onto FAITH.

Be the strong person you are, fall in love with yourself over and over again, no matter how bad it seems, you are worth living.

It gets easier with TIME. Give yourself time.

Give yourself time to heal.

Give yourself time to prove your worth.

Give yourself time to love again.

Give yourself time to trust.

Give yourself time for your appointed testimony.

"...because time and chances happen to them all" -[Ecc. 9:11]

Enjoy your youthful life with all the failures, mistakes and regrets.

CHAPTER 1

Boi! Boi! Boi! Came the loud wailing of the poor widow. Everyone could hear her heart-wrenching wails as far as the market square. What could have happened to make anyone cry this much on a hot afternoon? Her wails seemed too urgent to ignore, the villagers started to run toward the screams. No one could have anticipated the sight that met them when they got to her compound. Here was Maame rolling on the floor half-naked amidst loud wails and tears. The women in the little crowd that had gathered drew the little ones closer to themselves to prevent them from seeing the sorry and traumatic sight. The men could only stand akimbo at the doorway, trying to block the views of the women and children with their mouths agape.

This was a sight alien to the villagers. Even the strong-hearted men could not hide their worry at what they had just seen. Hanging from the ceiling was the now lifeless body of Nyamekye. From her neck, was a thick nylon rope commonly used as a clothesline in many homes.

Maame wailed more. Between her wails and tears, it was hard to make out what she tried to say. None of the onlookers could comfort this broken mother and widow.

"What did I do to deserve this?" she cried out.

"Mewuo oo (I'm dead)!! who plucked the only eye of this blind woman? Who has made me barren again? Who has taken the only dry bread from this widow's plate?" she continued in her wails.

"Oh! Mighty God, I thought I had a covenant with you!" she said as if to some unseen being in the room.

Turning to the lifeless body the men were trying to bring down from the ceiling, she cried,

"Why my dear, why? Why do you have to break your poor mother's heart like this? If you wanted to go, you should have told me, I would have gone with you!"

As if struck by someone, she fell to the floor screaming and demanding in anger, "Death please take me! I beg of you death, take me with her! Can you not open the gates of hell for me? Please!"

By this time, the women who could muster some courage to enter the room were trying desperately to cover Maame's nakedness and attempted comforting her. After several minutes of struggling, they managed to get her to sit on a small crooked stool they had found in the house.

The men had been able to finally bring down the lifeless body of her only daughter Nyamekye so the corpse could be transported to a burial site as their tradition demanded. This kind of death was unnatural and demanded that the earlier the corpse was buried, the faster the family could heal from their loss and it would deter others from following suit. Someone had called a taxi from the village centre and it had arrived at top speed bringing with it a trail of dust from the bumpy untarred road.

When the men started to move Nyamekye's body to the vehicle, Maame jumped up from the stool with fresh tears rolling down her cheeks amidst new wails. "What could have made you take your own life Nyamekye? If I didn't kill you when I conceived you, why will you take your own life?"

The men looked away, this sight could break the hearts of even the strong-willed men in the village. No parent should witness this sight, they thought. She kept wailing as she followed the corpse of her daughter being dumped in the car. She would not be allowed to go bury her daughter, the burial site would be unmarked. Taking your own life was the most dishonourable way to die as such a dishonourable burial is given to such death. This was going to be the last time she saw her daughter. None of the women could comfort Maame, then again, who could comfort a woman with such a tragic story.

One woman in the crowd said, "Ah! What is the matter with young people today? How could a young light be snuffed out this early? Why would a child take her own life?" Another woman replied, "is it not said that the sins of the father will visit the children, well here we are." As if by instinct the group unanimously responded "Ayoo!! (Indeed!)"

To deter other young people from following the same path, the village chief ordered that the corpse be buried that very day in an unmarked grave. This abomination should not be repeated. The corpse was ordered to be buried "like a dead animal". The men carried out this instruction all the while praying they nor their children would ever meet such a fate.

At Maame's compound, the crowd began to thin out. The gossips had started to discuss what possible motives there could have been for this tragic death. By the end of the day, people two villages over would have heard the news. This kind of news travelled fast although the farther it went, the more distorted it became. As the crowd left one by one to their own homes, they left in groups whispering to each other and shaking their heads at what had befallen Maame's home.

That night was as quiet as ever. Even the moon was hidden. For a village like Nyakotom, this was uncommon. Most nights, the sky was starry and the moon stood so bright that folks were seen gathered around campfires relaxing and conversing about the most trivial things. It was common to see children running around being chased by their siblings or mothers to go to bed while men smoked their pipes or drank around the fires talking. Tonight was different, it was not a night fit to make merry. An abomination had been committed in the village.

Maame lay on her bed still as a log. It was quite late but she could not close her eyes. They were red, swollen, and hurting but nothing could compare to the pain in her heart. She could feel her heart breaking over and over again when the image of her daughter's lifeless body hanging from the ceiling came to her mind as she tried closing her eyes.

In the hall were a few volunteering women who decided to stay the night to prevent her from harming herself in her grief. Almost no one had wanted to sleep in that house as many had decided it was cursed and haunted. The chief's wife being the leader of women in the village, had a tough time convincing a few older women to spend a few nights in Maame's house to make sure she was okay.

On such quiet nights, everyone should have been fast asleep but not the widow who had just lost her only daughter and child. She tossed and turned in her bed. By this time, she could no longer bring out tears. She was scared, confused, and still in disbelief. Maybe she was dreaming and the morning sun would cause her to wake up from this horrible nightmare, she thought in consolation. She closed her swollen eyes and recalled the men cutting the twisted rope from her daughter's neck. She could not even properly mourn her daughter and provide final rites for her daughter's passing. How could they expect her to just let go of her only joy in this wretched life? Did they not know without the final rites, her daughter would not have a guide to the afterlife?

She moaned softly, "My child is alone and afraid. Nyamekye, who will guide you to the afterlife? I pray your father meets you on the road to take you there so you do not get lost." She continued, "should I just follow her to guide her?"

Before she could keep that train of thought, sleep overtook her for it is said that sleep is as strong as death.

In a far-off distance, a cock in the village crowed. It was time to get up and go about the day's business. Maame woke up with a jolt. She was always up at the first crow to start her day early. Every day, she had to wake up her daughter who seemed to love to sleep more than any other thing in her life. She instinctively walked to her daughter's room knocked once and barged into the room to wake her up. The bed was unmade. "What is wrong with this girl always making me talk about making her bed first thing in the morning?", she murmured.

"Nyamekye! Nyamekye! It's too early for me to be shouting your name. Where are you?! How many times should I tell you to make your bed and at the very least tidy up your room? I am too old to do this for you." Two older women quickly rushed to Nyamekye's room. They had seen this many times when people lost their loved ones. The reality was too harsh for the mind to accept. "Who were these women and why were they in her house at this time of the day?", she thought. Suddenly, she remembered and collapsed. It had been one week after the suicide of her child and every morning, Maame woke up expecting to see her daughter in the room.

Maame had lost weight. She was not eating properly or sleeping. Everyone who passed by her compound and saw her sitting outside looked at her with pity. Others even pointed accusing fingers and the rest just gossiped trying to find possible reasons for this tragedy. Maame was a shadow of herself. Nothing made sense to her. She lashed out at the least provocation and laughed at nothing.

Two months on and the village seemed to have moved on, forgotten about the tragedy. Seeing the smiling faces of the villagers annoyed her to no end. "How can people be this wicked? How could they just move on as if everything was normal when I have lost everything? Does no one care at all? The most difficult part is that I cannot even talk to anyone about my daughter as it had been declared a taboo to even mention my daughter's name in public. Is Nyamekye going to be forgotten like she never even existed?" she said to herself.

As difficult as it was, Maame had tried to move on. She had wanted to accept the death of her young and energetic daughter but the guilt of being a mother who did not see her daughter's suffering was the worst part. That guilt lived with her. Worse off were the villagers who would whisper behind her back as she passed by. They had gradually alienated her so no one would attract whatever curse she carried.

They said she must have done something in the past to attract punishment from the gods. If not her sins, the sins of her forefathers must have caught up to her. Her daughter was now a yardstick used to advise and scare children and even women in the village.

"Is someone else going through this pain?" She thought.

CHAPTER 2

Maame sat in a pensive mood, her hands crossed over her chest. "Hmmmm", she sighed and put the last dress in her small traveling bag she had been packing for about a week. Catching a glimpse of an old photograph on her small dressing table, she walked across the room and picked up the photograph. Those were happy times. Frozen in time was a photograph of her perfect family; her husband, her only daughter, and herself smiling from ear to ear. How did her life move from that point to this? How had she become a widow and a grieving mother at such a young age? She could not bring herself to take along the photograph. It was a grim reminder that she had lost everything.

She placed it back down with a heavy heart and turned away as if trying to avoid the gazes of the happy family in that photo. She walked to her bed where her packed bag was and looked around the room in one final sweep. Looking at that picture had brought back painful memories.

She had met her husband at an early age and had fallen in love so quickly. The problem was that he was much older than she was and this often brought up arguments between her parents and herself. Her parents had been adamant that a thirty-year age gap was too much to comprehend. "What kind of love could be that blind?", her mother once said in a heated argument. Against all odds and with a half blessing from her parents, she got married to him anyway.

During the first few years of the marriage, she endured four miscarriages and on the fifth one, she almost took her own life. That traumatic experience of surviving the suicide attempt made her vow never to do that again. It was not just because of the miscarriages that drove her to commit this act. The miscarriages in themselves were not so bad because her husband had been supportive throughout the times of joy and the times of loss. Her parents and peers summed up her problems.

They had made her into a theme of gossip. Her marriage and miscarriages were easily the hottest topics of gossip among her peers. To make matters worse, her parents never missed a chance to remind her of how stubborn she was. "Well, the only thing we can do now is to pray that God or even a smaller god shows you some favour, and gifts you with a child. Perhaps you now see the sense in what we had been saying all this while" her mother had said after the third miscarriage. "Why you would marry a man old enough to be your father is still beyond me. God is not blind to the insolence of children towards their parents Maame, and I know you are paying for that sin", her mother continued.

Rumour had it that, she had insisted on marrying the old man not for love, but for the large cocoa farm he possessed and would not allow him to take another wife. She was on the verge of giving up on having children when she took seed again. Was this going to be like the others? She had thought when she found out. Throughout the pregnancy, she was waiting for when she would miscarry. After six months, she started to have a little faith that she would be able to see this child alive. After all, she was praying her growing seed would be stubborn enough not to give up and die. Her husband treated her like a queen. No work for her, no strenuous activities, and definitely no going out to attract unwanted attention. The elderly man everyone had mocked for having "weak sperms" was going to be a father.

At eight months, Maame had to make her husband vow not to buy another gift for her. She had been showered with too many gifts and there was almost no room to put some of them. "Let's save some of the gifts for the baby, haba!", she mockingly exclaimed to her husband. This was a man she would marry all over again if she was to reincarnate. He was wealthy not because he had inherited some property but because he was hardworking. Growing up, Agya her husband had learnt to farm from his parents who owned a small piece of land in their backyard. His father never missed a day on the farm with the saying, "the day you don't go is the day you have begun to lose your farm. Be consistent!" That had become Agya's motto too. He had expanded his cocoa farm by buying nearby farms and had even started to rear animals for their consumption. Meat was never scarce in their home and Maame's fat cheeks were enough proof. He had vowed to provide the world for this woman who defended him to her parents and friends. He took her hand in his big and calloused palm from all the farmwork. He had told her time and again "I want to make you the envy of all women", Maame would smile and reply, "I already am".

Maame was the only woman in the small village to have a maidservant because Agya would not allow her to lift a finger to work. After nine months, they welcomed their baby girl,

Nyamekye (God's gift). Since she was a Monday born, she took on the local name Adjoa. At home, the name Adjoa was only heard when she showed her stubborn or rebellious side. Agya always attributed that to her mother. Nyamekye was her pet name when they needed her to run errands or she had done a good deed.

When Nyamekye had turned ten, someone accidentally started a fire on Agya's farm after they left a burning tire used to trap bush rats on the farmland. The fire consumed almost everything. Some boys who saw the big fire ran to tell Agya who rushed to the scene. He tried to save his farm. This was years of his hard work going up in flames. He called for help but no one seemed to be coming. He tried to quench the huge fire himself. By the time the fire died down, he had inhaled too much smoke for his aging lungs. He collapsed and was rushed to the hospital. Sadly, he was pronounced dead on arrival. He had left behind a beautiful young wife and an even more beautiful daughter. Maame had to be strong for her daughter. She knew she would have to be a pillar of support for her daughter who loved her father so much. Maame even vowed to never take another man although she had a lot of suitors coming her way. Her daughter was the only thing that mattered to her and nothing would replace that.

Nyamekye was now in high school. Her first year in school was not easy because she was to live in a boarding house with several other girls while being far away from any and everything she knew. These new girls had come from different backgrounds with most coming from the city where the school was located. Their provisions, clothing, language, and mannerisms were all new to her. Even the food served at school was new to her. She missed home.

At home, she would usually have a heavy meal in the morning which would take her halfway through the day. Here, she was served a very light breakfast which left her hungry again by mid-morning. The school was also strict on cutlery use. She was required to use a fork and a knife at the dining table whereas there were several days she ate with her hands at home. The first day at the school's dining hall was the most embarrassing she had felt all her life. She had dropped her knife on the floor creating a loud clanging noise that drew all eyes to her. When she apologized and tried to pick up the knife, her fork which was not properly placed on her plate also fell. This was her first night and she knew everyone would now remember her by that scene. She was half done with the food and hungry, but with no spare cutlery to eat the remaining food, she left the food and went back to the dormitory hungry. That night at the dorm, she became a topic that the other girls in the dormitory could bond over. They laughed so hard at her that she went to bed far earlier than the time set to sleep. She cried into her pillow silently and remembered her parents. She missed both of them now, especially her father.

Nyamekye had been one of the three girls selected by their Junior high school with a scholarship to study in one of the best high schools in the country, making her mother and even her community proud. The joy she felt leaving the small village for the city was replaced with sorrow at not fitting in the school. She was finding it hard to fit in and making friends was even harder because she could not speak the "good English" that showed you came from a good home or a good school. She had lost all self-confidence and she was lagging behind in her school work as well. Everything was moving too fast for her.

After the long and dreadful first year, vacation had come and she could finally go home. She promised herself she would not come back to the school the next academic year and no one was going to convince her to come back to this hell. There was a school in a neighbouring town and she had made up her mind to transfer there. That conversation with her mom did not go well. Her mom would not even hear of it. Her mom insisted that she had got an opportunity that comes to very few people once in a lifetime and won't allow her stubbornness to ruin it.

A new year had begun and it was worse. After the vacation, new trends hit. Social media had allowed the other girls to stay in touch and even hang out on some days. Nyamekye had been left out of this because she did not have a clue as to how social media even worked. In fact, her mother had promised to get her a phone only after she completed secondary school and Nyamekye had been of the view all parents did the same.

The bullying had become worse because the other girls seemed to be good friends. New girls had also come to school as juniors. She concluded that the only way to get back at them was with academics. If she could surpass them, they would have no way to talk like that to her. They would need her to help them with their academics. That started well until one day at the mass Assembly grounds, Nyamekye's school uniform had accidentally ripped. What had happened? she thought as the girls standing behind her started to giggle and call the attention of other girls. Suddenly everyone was laughing hysterically even the juniors who were normally afraid to look at their seniors. As a mixed school (co-ed) both girls and boys needed to meet at the grounds for the mass Assembly. It was at such a place that her dress had decided to rip. As to how it had happened, Nyamekye could not even remember. She just wanted to vanish at that moment. She left the assembly grounds and for about a week had missed all her classes. When all seemed lost, there was a glimmer of hope, or so she had thought.

One of the "cool girls" from her year group had invited her to join them one afternoon for lunch, as surprised as she was, she was still excited. These girls were the cool ones. Everyone wanted to be their friends but they were very selective about who they brought into their circle. They did things that were easily considered taboo in Nyamekye's home. But their daring attitudes and even waywardness were something every student admired to an extent. Well, they were the richest in the school and a word from their parents combined could easily shut down the school forever. No teacher wanted to be the one to punish such kids.

Nyamekye just needed friends, she just wanted anyone to talk to her without remarking about the several embarrassing incidents or her bad English. She was ready to do anything simply to belong. At the lunch, Nyamekye just knew she was in a bad crowd when they made statements like "there was no fun being a good girl" and told her their dream was to leave a mark in school so everyone would remember them. Not the good mark but the bad one that makes people spin outrageous stories about these "heroes".

They were crazy Nyamekye thought and she

was even crazier to sit here with them. One girl had even managed to bring out a bottle of alcohol to lunch. How on earth did they get alcohol within the four walls of this school? At the gate, all provisions were checked at the start of the term to make sure any 'contraband' was seized. Even Nyamekye's slippers given to her as a gift from her mother were seized because the teacher had said it was "too shiny" to be considered a simple slipper. How then did alcohol pass right under their nose?

Another boy in the cool group remarked "I hope you aren't as naïve as you look dear" and winked. The rest of the group broke out in a fit of laughter. She was determined to fit in and took the bottle taking a deep swig of its contents. She did not expect that burning sensation in her throat at the first gulp. How did people get drunk on this bitter and burning liquid? she thought. She passed the bottle back to the leader. If this was what it took to be a "cool girl" she was ready to do it.

Sitting across the teacher's desk was Nyamekye in her green and white uniform well above her knees and too short to pass the decency code in the school. What had happened to the clumsy girl he knew in her first year? The teacher stared at the cold face of the sixteen-year-old girl that was trying so hard to cover her exposed thighs. "How did we get here?" he asked. She gave a shrug to show she did not know and did not care. She looked away and he continued, "I only wish you did not have to change so much Nyamekye".

Nothing could shoot down her happiness. Nyamekye after hanging out with the "cool group" had become one of the most popular members of the group. She was beautiful and that stole the hearts of her secret fans. She was no longer the clumsy girl who smelled funny and could barely look anyone in the eyes. This Nyamekye was confident and now had an equally handsome boyfriend. He was in every sense of the word a "bad boy" but he made her happy. He told her she was the most beautiful woman he had ever seen and spoke to her in a way that no man had ever done. This was indeed love, she thought. They would both miss classes to enjoy their own company in their favourite secret spot. That continued absence was why she had been called to her teacher's office. He had just told her, that the scholarship she came to school with had been canceled because of her non-performance but she did not seem to care. After all, her friends were the richest in the school and so was her boyfriend, they could easily help her out. Having cool friends she thought, was more important.

After the talk with her teacher, she did not feel right. She needed to see her boyfriend. He was the only one who could make her feel better at this point. They met at their usual spot and this time she decided to give in to her emotions. After all, he was worth it. They started to caress and things quickly escalated. Before she knew it, he had undressed her and was making love to her on the bare floor. This was her first time and she felt magical. How come she had not tried this earlier? Why had her mother warned her so much about having sex at her age? That night she was the happiest she had ever been.

Sitting nervously under the "lover's tree" as this lover's hotspot was secretly called, Nyamekye was almost in tears. It had been six weeks now and she had not seen her monthly period. Something was wrong. It could be a disease she thought but then brushed off the thought when she added the other symptoms she had been experiencing. A girl in the dormitory had shared a story of a senior colleague who got pregnant while in school and how she had to be sacked and humiliated. The symptoms described were the same. Headaches, morning sickness, tiredness, and most importantly missed periods. She suspected she was pregnant and there was only one person this pregnancy belonged to. He was coming to meet her now.

After breaking the news to him, a heated argument ensued. "Me, impregnate you?", he asked in a menacing voice. "I don't think you are right in your head Nyamekye. Or is it because we hang out?"

"Hang out? Did you say hang out? Were we not dating George? Did we not –" her words were cut short.

"Listen here," he said as he clamped a hand over her mouth before she could scream out the last few words, "I don't know what you are talking about. If you claim I impregnated you bring a witness otherwise don't even dare to pin this on me. If you go around with that story I will make you sorry."

She could not believe what she was hearing. She had watched movies where the man would carry the lady in his arms after she told him of the pregnancy. That was what she was expecting. She had fantasised about telling him this "good news" and how in his excitement, he would go down on one knee asking her to be his wife. They would get married and settle down starting their life as a young married couple blessed with a baby. Maybe after the birth of the child, she would pick up a trade while George found some office work in his father's company. Things were perfectly planned out in her fantasy, but what was happening now? Why was she standing here with the father of her child acting like she got pregnant on her own?

His voice broke through her thoughts. "If I hear this story on the lip of any student in this school, I am walking straight to administration and reporting that you are a slut who sleeps around with boys and that you are trying to pin a pregnancy on me. I will have my friends add their voices as well. You know my Father –" he continued fuming, "I will make your life miserable if you try that nonsense Nyamekye!" By now he was screaming at her, other students passing by wondered what love quarrel these lovebirds were having.

Before he walked away he turned and said "I can't believe you thought I was dating an ugly person like yourself". He laughed hysterically and walked away. In a not-so-far-off distance were his friends. When he got to them he spoke to them and although she couldn't hear what he said, it must not have been a good statement because they had laughed so hard at her. They walked off towards the basketball field to have a game like they normally did completely ignoring her.

Nyamekye was in shock. She was frozen at the spot looking at his retreating back for what seemed to be like forever before her tears clouded her vision and brought her back to reality. She walked straight to her dorm. She packed a few things and made up her mind she would rather die than go through this embarrassment on her own. She had lost her scholarship and was pregnant. She could not face her mother in this shame. What had she done? Maybe a reincarnation would give her the chance to start afresh. She believed this.

When she got home, her mother was not at home. Her mother did not know she was coming home anyway. She wanted to write down a note, but she could not think of anything to pen down. A sorry note? A thank you note? What should she say to the mother who had been prepared to sell the very clothes on her back to give Nyamekye a comfortable life? Maybe there was a god who could help her undo her foolishness with a second chance in life. But was there such a chance? There was only one way to find out. She climbed the table in the centre of the living room and hang herself in her tears.

CHAPTER 3

Maame boarded the bus going to the city. She had said nothing to anyone on her way to board the bus and said nothing throughout the three-hour journey. She wanted to be left alone with her thoughts. The last time she had ventured on the bus to the city was to see her daughter at school. Today, however, she was going to the city for a very different reason.

"Last stop!!!" came the loud voice of the driver waking Maame and some other napping passengers from their slumber. Opening her eyes, the scorching sun pierced her eyes, causing her to shut them again. There were hawkers, and a crowd of people at the bus station bustling about. The crowd was a mix of taxi drivers trying to get the attention of prospective passengers, hawkers shouting out their wares, and head porters balancing loads on their heads in the most intriguing way. Mixed within this noisy crowd were the horns and revving engines of buses as they came to drop passengers or left for their journeys.

This noise was the reason she never fancied the big city. She alighted from the bus, clutching her traveling bag tightly, and stood still trying to get her bearings. She had come to see her good friend, Linda in the big city. Linda had asked her to come to the big city because she was not convinced Maame should stay in the village all alone after the traumatic passing of her daughter. This friend had been with her through thick and thin. This was someone Maame knew she could rely on. The only reason Maame had decided to take up the offer of a visit to the city was because of a help group Linda had insisted she joined. "Try and come here for a week and give this group a chance. If it does not help after a week, you are free to leave", Maame recalled her saying. After a quick call to her friend, directions were given and Maame made her way to the house she would be hosted in for the next few weeks.

"I don't think I can live through this. My heart aches and my thoughts are always running wild" Maame said after they had sat down to chat later that evening. "Am I still considered a mother,

Linda? I ask myself if I would ever get to be called granny, attend graduation ceremonies or even hand over a child in marriage. These are the thoughts that are always tormenting me."

Linda gave her a bear hug. "I don't know how long it will take Maame, but you will be fine. I know this and I promise", she whispered. "I already informed them you'll be there tomorrow. I only insist on this group because I have seen the results from others and myself particularly after the demise of my parents when I thought I could not go on in life." She continued, "It always gets better with time. It always does." Maame was by now bawling out her pain. She knew she needed help quickly before she harmed herself or others around her.

Slowly she walked into the room filled with strangers. Linda could have given her a heads up at the very least about the number of people that attended these meetings Maame thought. Linda had said she estimated about four (4) people came to the meetings and it was kept very private. Why then were about twenty people filling this small room? Each person sitting there looked perfectly fine. What could have driven these wealthy-looking people to come here. Stealing glances around the room, she decided to make the best of this support group even if it meant making these strangers her friends. Her nervousness would not prevent her from attaining her goal. She sat down and looked at the sad décor the organisers seemed to have hung around to bring cheer to the moody room. There was nothing cheerful in the room save a bubbly thin lady who seemed to be the leader of the group.

She went around trying to greet everyone with a smile that made Maame think would cause her cheeks to hurt. Her hands flew around at every word she said and it was a surprise she had not hit anyone yet. Everyone tried to reciprocate her cheerfulness but most couldn't. After all, they came there not because they were happy to be there but because they all admitted they needed help one way or the other. When the lady got to her, Maame was hit with the smell of flowers from the lady's perfume. She was the type of lady that could light up a room easily and one whose absence would be severely felt. Maame tried to cut the pleasantries short but this was a lady who was determined to make a long conversation.

"Hi my dear!" the lady chirped, "you must be Maame. Oh! Your good friend told me about you and I have been expecting you. In fact we all have," she said extending her hand to indicate the entire group had been expecting to see Maame there. Maame looked around but the blank faces of the group members told her they neither cared for her presence nor absence.

"Thank you", Maame said politely

"Oh don't thank me. I should thank you. You have taken the first bold step. Many do not get to take this step. But you have and you chose none other than Mrs. Mona's support group" she went on. By this time, Maame was praying this chirpy lady would find another victim to torment because she was not one to hold conversations for long, especially with loud, chirpy, and overly cheerful strangers. As if by queue, the lady Mrs. Mona stood up from where she had taken a seat by Maame to start the meeting. "No time to waste" she whispered and winked at Maame while she made her way to the front of the room.

At the corner of the room by the door was a man tall and dark. He had a certain air of mystery to him and looked unattentively at everything going on. It seemed like he was forced to be there and would not miss any opportunity to leave through the door he was sitting by. Maame later learned he was Mr. Mona, husband to the cheerful lady, and was always present at the meeting not because he liked to be there but because he loved his wife and everything she did. Rumor had it that the one day he missed the meeting was the day Mrs. Mona was less chirpy. Indeed it seems the opposites do attract.

During the opening prayer, with Maame's eyes closed, she heard a little scuffle by her side which sounded like someone trying to find a seat. Then she smelled alcohol which forced her to open her eyes. Here was a man in his late forties or early fifties drunk as a skunk with a bottle of liquor in his hands trying to keep himself from falling over in his seat. What could his story have been to walk into this support group drunk? He looked educated and a good shower and clean shave would have brought out his true beauty. The meeting had started and with that, people took turns to introduce themselves and share their stories.

CHAPTER 4

Andrew's Story

Andrew was a young energetic young man described by most of his friends as the perfect boy. He was born and raised in one of the few wealthy families in the country and he generally enjoyed the good life. His family's wealth originated from his grandfather's business who was at a point awarded the best timber farmer in the country. His grandfather was the first exporter of timber to other countries and for a long time was the sole exporter. This wealth allowed for his mother to be trained as the best and most sought-after surgeon in the country and West Africa. Some said she had the very hands of God bringing people back from the brink of death.

Andrew was thus raised to succeed at all costs. He could either be a businessman taking after the numerous family businesses or have a career in medicine like his mother. Either way, his life was paved with gold from the very start. He never failed in class, how could he? He had the best teachers as private tutors with some holding Ph.D.s in their fields. To his parents, having all these resources meant he had no excuse to fail. Even a second position in the entire class was considered a failure. "What head does Martin who came first have that you do not have Andrew? His mother is a trader and I hear he does not even attend the extra classes organized at the school because they cannot afford it. So what is your excuse for coming in second?" his mother had said after he came second one particular term.

After his primary education, he was moved to a private school. His parents believed a private school would give him the best resources to study harder than anyone. He excelled in his academics but something was amiss. He wanted to sing. He wanted to be a musician. During one vacation, he had dared to speak to his parents about it and they dismissed the matter so much, that it was forbidden for him to bring up "such nonsense" as they had said in their house. His mother decided the life of business would give him too much leeway to do whatever he wanted and bring shame to the family seeing as how he wanted to be a musician. They then concluded his career would be in the medical field. He would be a doctor or a surgeon and the best this country had, to the point of surpassing her. It was no surprise then when he gained admission into a medical school outside the country to begin training for his career.

For the very first time since he started school, Andrew failed his exams. He was given two more chances to re-write the exams and in all those chances, he failed again and again. The school recommended that he went to his home country to rejuvenate and connect with family as it might help him get back on his feet. The school had admitted him because of this track record of academic success and so it was a shock to see this kind of failure from an excelling student.

That decision to go back home took a turn for the worst. Instead of coming to a supportive family, his father could not stop screaming at him telling Andrews how much he had embarrassed the entire family with his failure. "If you want to fail and embarrass yourself, you should have done it in a family that is not ours. But with all our pride on the line, you decided to single-handedly drag my face in the mud right? You decided that you would choose the path to dishonor your parents by coming back a failure. Did you think you will come home to hugs and a party? You better get yourself together to return to that school on the next flight. Do you know how much money is going into your schooling boy?!" He had never seen his father this enraged before. But this was not as worse as what Andrew faced with his mother that evening after she returned from work. Did no one care how he was feeling from all this pressure? His father had already booked a flight back to the school leaving the next morning but Andrew had decided the only body that will fly back would be his dead body.

That evening, he went to the pharmacy and bought several pills. He went back home and took them all. Even as a failed medical student, he knew the right combination of drugs to get his heart to stop and that was what he did.

"No! No! No!" came the loud wailing of his mother at the sight of her dead son with the container of the pills he took lying by his side. She had come to take him to the airport but the silence in the bedroom had prompted her to use her master key to open his bedroom door.

She screamed, she rolled on the floor, she could not be comforted. Her prized child had taken his own life. She could not get over the image she saw that day. Once the best surgeon, she could not go back to work. The once happy home had been torn apart.

Andrews's death had brought a blame game to the family. While the parents blamed each other, the remaining siblings blamed their parents. The sadder thing was that Andrews' other siblings had been ignored as their parents focused their attention on the success of the first child Andrew. His death collapsed the marriage of his parents and broke the family apart. The fight for property among the family members had brought the family to an irreparable state.

The pretty woman in her mid-forties recounting her story reached into her purse and brought out a crumpled note. She read;

You are a good mother,

You did great, I am just taking the lead Mom

Love you forever.

She smiled sadly as a tear rolled down her cheek and said "this is my story", before taking her seat. Maame nodded and thought how happy she would have been if Nyamekye had penned down a note. If only she had a piece of paper from her daughter, she would have healed better.

As the woman sat, she looked right at Maame as if gesturing for her to share her story. Everyone turned to look at Maame. She shook her head violently. "I don't think I am ready to share my story yet," she said in a tone barely a whisper almost as if telling herself. Mrs. Mona replied as she always did with the new members, "take all the time you need and keep coming here. Maybe one day we would hear what brought you here so it encourages someone too."

CHAPTER 5

Hearing stories from the other members of the group week after week helped Maame realise there were people in possibly worse predicaments than she was going through. At least, she concluded that it was not a curse passed down from her father or grandfather for that matter. Her predicament was not a result of a sin she had committed in her past life or her past. She was not a bad mother or an unfortunate wife. She had done her best. She had given her daughter the best she could, given their standing in life. Life had dealt her bad cards but she had still kept her head in the game.

Weeks of therapy saw her looking more cheerful and better prepared to face each day, unlike her past self. She had hated seeing the new day dawn, as it had reminded her of her daily morning routine of waking her daughter up to go sweep and tidy up the compound. Now she woke up feeling less resentful of the rising sun and actually looking forward to Mrs. Mona's chirpy attitude. She had begun to heal and that for her was something she had thought almost impossible.

Mrs. Mona had tasked them that week to face their sorrows head-on by putting away painful reminders of their past. For Maame that meant going back to the village and tidying up Nyamekye's room. Ever since her daughter's passing, she had not gathered the courage to tidy up the room and dispose of things that were not of use anymore. She made up her mind to set off and informed her friend.

The very next day Maame was on the bus on the way back to the village. As she stared at the road speeding past her, her thoughts strayed to the time she had boarded a bus to the city and in what state of mind she had been in. She looked at her reflection in the window pane. She had begun to gain weight again evidenced by her fattening cheeks. The frown lines on her brows had begun to recede and she had generally begun to look younger and better. Sorrow does indeed bother the soul and the body as well, she thought.

Walking from the bus station to her own home which was not so far, she could see the rooftop of her house. The bright blue aluminum sheets she remembered telling Agya to change for her. She had fancied a red colour but Agya had insisted on the blue roof with a promise he would change it to her preferred colour after 5 years. That promise could not be fulfilled with him in the ground. She looked elsewhere, trying to stop the occasional tear that threatened to fall every time she thought of her husband or child.

Her compound was well organized and neatly kept save the few leaves lying around the compound. No utensils or domestic tools were lying around as is commonly seen in other homes. She always insisted on keeping her compound neat because she believed it founded the perception of any visitor entering her home. A disorganized compound would give the impression that the occupants of the house were lazy and disorganized. She had therefore always made sure to neatly stash away all brooms, utensils, domestic tools, etc

She went inside and settled on her bed. The trip from the big city was not particularly tiring, but the thought of what she had to do drained her of her energy. "We cannot seek to achieve everything in one day. Tomorrow may not be promised to me but at least I can schedule this assignment for the morning," she justified her procrastination.

The very next morning, she was up bright and early. She would not postpone or procrastinate what she had to do. She went into her daughter's room along with the bags she had brought. She had decided to not waste the dresses by burning them but to give them away. Nyamekye had an eye for fashion and Maame did not know when to stop showering her daughter with gifts of clothes. This relationship had lead Nyamekye to amass a lot of clothes some of which had their tags and others looking like they had been worn only once. Maame separated the clothes into each bag; those that will go to the young girls of Nyamekye's age and those articles that were too personal to give away and would need to be burned.

Maame had contacted some women who had daughters of Nyamekye's age and had told them to come by for the clothes. After packing the clothes, she waited and waited later realizing they would not come. The women had forbidden their daughters from taking any clothing or gift from Maame claiming that they were cursed. Rumours had spread of Maame's supposed goodwill with many claiming she was trying to spread her curse to other people's homes. Realising she was still regarded as a curse in the village, she proceeded to burn all the clothes and items because no one would want to come near her house or even take any thing she was freely offering them. These were the same people who came to her house day and night seeking help from herself and her husband.

It had been exactly a year since her daughter's death and Maame knew by custom that it was time to organize the anniversary of the passing of her daughter. She went to the village chief and pleaded with him to show her where her daughter had been buried. She only needed to perform the traditional rights of praying for her soul. The chief agreed and gave her some young men to guide her to the site. It was a far-off distance and quite dangerous for a woman to trek on her own. Getting to the burial site was not easy. The road was barely marked out and it was overgrown with shrubs, thorns, and weeds. The trees in this part of the village were huge casting deep shadows on the path. By the time they got to the burial site, the young men were grumbling in anger over how far they had to walk. Maame pressed a few coins into their palms hoping it would calm them down. It didn't. They looked at the coins, looked at the woman, and just walked away without thanking Maame. She said nothing. She was used to worse.

The site of her daughter's burial was just a small mound overgrown with weeds. She brought the hoe she had carried along and began to weed around the site. She then went around picking up the nicest stones close by and arranged them neatly around the burial site. This was the very least she could do to give her daughter a decent burial site. On the largest stone piece she placed at the head of the mound, she inscribed on it "LOVED DEARLY".

When she stood up she looked at her handiwork and smiled. She gave a deep sigh and made a small prayer for her daughter's soul. Indeed it is a curse for a parent to bury their child. That is just not right. Maame took out the small lunch she had packed and began to eat it as she remembered fondly sharing a meal with her daughter. After that, she got up to leave. She felt better, indeed she still had unanswered questions about why her child took her own life, and she may never find the answers she needed. But today she could go back knowing she had done one good thing for her daughter to rest more peacefully.

She walked back on the long winding road overgrown with weeds and shrubs on each side. Buried in her thoughts she did not realise how far she had walked. She found herself walking almost robotically towards her house. She passed by a few women who walked by stealing glances at her and gossiping about her. She laughed out at this. This made her think of the story a white couple shared at the last meeting she partook.

She remembered her shock at seeing whites for the first time in person and more importantly at a support group meant for broken people. From the movies she had seen, these whites had therapists or supportive friends to open up to. Little did she know that this was far from reality.

"Our hearts broke the very day our baby left us and it still breaks to date," said the white lady whose name was MaryAnn. Because of her heavy American accent, everyone strained their ears trying to hear every single word they said or at least the meaning of the sentences. "I still shed tears talking about our golden boy. His name was Adam." She said softly causing everyone to draw a little closer to them. "Adam was born on a hot August afternoon in Las Vegas. His blonde hair and tiny fingers stole our hearts immediately." She looked at her husband, "never did I know I could love another person more than myself. I would have given my very life to him if it came to it." She paused to sip water from a water bottle she had been fidgeting with.

"I told my husband here John –" pointing at her husband seated by her "- we are done with having any more children. It was traumatic enough the whole birthing process and how we struggled to conceive. As supportive as he is, he readily agreed. Looking back, I think I was being selfish." She reminisced.

Adam was the name of their son. He had been an active boy since the day he was born and was involved in all sporting activities in his school. Going to high school, Adam had decided to scale down and focus on basketball since he had identified his talent in that area. He had even won a couple of awards at high school tournaments. With the last-minute wins he always seemed to get his team, he was nicknamed the "golden boy".

The white lady had smiled sadly when she said this nickname. When Adam got to eleventh grade (the equivalent of SHS two in Ghana), she recounted how several colleges had proposed scholarships to her son given his talent in basketball. The choice of the college would ultimately determine the success of their basketball team and also his career path. It was a crucial point in a young man's life. She spoke with pride about how her golden boy Adam had still managed to graduate with honours with a 3.8 GPA score which was almost unheard of for a sport-focused person. After graduation, he had already decided on a college to join based on their track record of notable basketball talents that they had trained.

She struggled to continue although, at this juncture, it seemed harder for her to go on. "It was at college that everything took a turn for the worst", she fumed. "In his first year, he pushed himself so hard trying to balance out his grades with his games. The most unfortunate thing happened when he broke his ankle at a game and for the pain, he was prescribed hard drugs under strict orders to never overdose or over-rely on them. As time went on, however, he could not go a day without them", she said. Trying to control the tears that had welled up in her eyes, she requested a tissue from the host Mrs. Mona who had without realizing it left the front of the meeting to hear the story of this white woman. Mrs. Mona quickly took from her purse a portable tissue packet and handed it over. After some minutes, the woman was ready to go on. Everyone by now was at the edge of their seats hanging on to every word this woman was saying. To them, it was both strange to see a white woman at their meeting and one who looked broken. To some extent, it comforted them knowing that life happened to everyone regardless of their colour, race, or social status.

When she had recomposed herself, she went on. "My baby, Adam could not get off the drugs. He had wanted to prove himself worthy and without waiting for the ankle to fully heal, he had continued to train under the influence of the drug. He began to forge his doctor's signature to get more drugs for the increasing pain. When he was caught by the doctor, he decided that he would get the drugs from the streets if he could not get them the right way. All this while, we had no idea what our boy was doing. The doctor had not even told us of this forgery until later. We would have given him the help he needed if we had seen this on time. It did not have to escalate. Only if he had spoken, but I blame myself. I was not an attentive mother. I should have seen my baby's struggle and pain."

She screamed suddenly as if trying to vent out some pain she had locked up for so long. Maame had remembered how she used to blame her poor parenting skills for not seeing the pain of her child Nyamekye. But what could she have done when children had become better at hiding their secrets, Mrs. Mona had told her in one of her meetings.

"His addiction prevented him from performing his best at games. His coach had noticed his unusual behavior and had him tested for drugs which came back positive. His scholarship was revoked, he was sacked from his team and he was sacked from school. In all of this, he never told us this. For months, he had been leaving home under the pretense of going to school only to join a gang of addicts. His records showed that he had tried to get into other schools using the old scholarships they had given him but he was denied because he had a tainted record", she was thoughtful at this point. "I guess his frustration and not wanting to let us down led him to take his own life. He must have thought taking his own life would end his suffering, what he forgot was that it would create our suffering. Why do they do this, huh? Why do they think taking their life would end things for them and forget that they are leaving others to grieve their passing? This is the worst kind of suffering. To make a mother bury her son and only child. After all we had done for him?!" She was screaming now at no one in particular. "How could these kids be so ungrateful forgetting that we have to watch them being lowered into the grave never to see them smile and never to hear their voice? If this is not the height of selfishness, I don't know what is!" Everyone nodded in agreement.

It had got Maame thinking, she always blamed herself forgetting how selfish Nyamekye had been as well. This woman was right, should suicide be the answer when things are tough? Did these kids even think of the sorrows their parents would go through after they had taken their lives? "May no other parent have to go through what we have gone through", Maame silently prayed heading back to her home to pack for the city. She had completed her task and was ready to go back to the city to continue her therapy.

CHAPTER 6

Back at the meeting, new faces had joined but it still felt like home. They had been sharing their stories with ease now. Everyone felt this was a space they could bare their scars without fear of stigma. Some stories cut to the heart and left everyone in tears. Others told their stories masking them with comedy that released some tension in the room. In all of it, the needed support was there for everyone and every member in the room could feel it. After Maame understood that frustration drove people to take their lives, she decided to get better quickly and educate others on the dangers of suicidal thoughts. It always began with a thought and progressed to the act. People in her small village had even thought it was a curse handed down and so at a point had brought a pastor to come deliver her from the curse in her family otherwise she might commit one herself. She shook her head to clear the memory.

Mrs Mona was bringing the meeting to an end. When a hand shot up. It was the man who was always drunk. Today he looked different. He had a clean shave and looked calmer than he usually did. For the first time, although he had his bottle of alcohol, he did not reek of it. It seemed he had not taken a single sip. With his hand still in the air, he said "I want to tell my story now. I think I am ready." Mrs Mona looked at the clock at the opposite end of the room indicating that the time for the meeting was up. Someone in the crowd said, "it's okay we can wait for a while longer." Heads nodded around the room in agreement indicating that they were willing to stay to hear his story and Mrs Mona motioned him to come to the front.

He looked younger now, with a good skin tone, and a nice tuxedo hinting at some wealth he must have. He also had a small pot belly which may have been from drinking Maame concluded. He could easily have been in his late forties or early fifties. He cleared his throat and began his story, cutting through Maame's thoughts.

"I married for love and we were deeply in love when we married young. Susan was a beautiful and intelligent young lady. We could not go a day without seeing each other. That was how strong our love for each other was. It felt as if we breathed one air and understood each other. We completed each other's sentences. So right after our university days, we decided to get married because we were both from strong conservative families. I especially was from a political family while Suzy as I affectionately called her was from an average home. I was from a rich, powerful and famous family and part of the lucky few", he said with a cocky smile. Maame lifted her head to get a closer look at this man thinking hard to recall if she had seen him anywhere before now. She shook her head and gave a little giggle, "I'm silly, where would our worlds have crossed seeing as I am from a poor home and he is a rich kid" she muttered to herself.

Focusing back on the man standing in front of the group, he took a sip of whatever was in the flask. After pulling a chair from the front and getting himself comfortable, he continued. "I remember the very first day Suzy walked into the lecture hall, she was a bit late and maybe it was intentional as I had come to realise with time. She was fair and her hair had been braided very long to her waist. She had wide eyes and a pointed nose with full lips to match. She was tall and slender but with wide hips. I remember the first time I set eyes on her like it was yesterday. She had heels and clasped in her hands a few books. Her top was cropped and paired with a mini-skirt and she loudly chewed on her gum while her heels made loud noises as she passed by the lecturer to take her seat. She had drawn all attention in the lecture theatre but looked as if she had no care in the world. It may sound crazy but right there and then, I knew that was my wife and the mother of my children - she was going to be 'my forever'. Yes, I wrote that on a piece of paper and passed it to her. She turned to look at me with those beautiful eyes and the most beautiful smile I had ever seen revealing a perfect set of white teeth. I muttered under my breath that this was the perfect creature. God had indeed taken His time to make this one."

He continued when he realized he had got everyone's rapt attention, "After a full semester of saying 'no' to all my proposals, she finally agreed to date me and that was it. We were never apart again," he paused, "or so I thought." The man took a deep sigh and continued.

"We got married right after university and our life as a married couple began. Everything was like a fairy tale. I knew the curveball was to come I just didn't know when. We lived a good life and two years into our marriage, God blessed us with two wonderful baby girls back to back. I suggested that my wife stop working and become a stay-at-home mom and she readily agreed with no argument. Come to think of it, we hardly ever argued. My home must have been the ideal home. I made sure my wife and the kids lacked nothing. We were practically the envy of our friends and family. We went on expensive vacations and enjoyed life as a family in the full glare of an envious world. Six years down the lane, I got my first diplomatic assignment outside the country and had to move my family. My Suzy was by my side yet again. She helped me by hosting all the parties for the high in society as I made more connections at such parties. Indeed we met and dined with the world's best, and my diplomatic assignments took us around the world to about thirty countries if I recall right and every single continent."

He continued although a bit reluctant, "my girls, my babies, grew up and went on living their lives while I decided to come back home to settle down. I looked forward to many more years with my wife but the devil had apparently scheduled other plans for me. At a point, I thought nothing bad could ever happen to me and believed that I must have been a part of the few lucky ones brought into this world."

At this point, Maame began to wonder who had been killed, or who had killed who and why, after all this meeting was for those with these issues. It was not a meeting for telling great life stories. The man stood up and it looked like this was going to be one long story and a long day today. He walked to stand behind the chair and continued. "I came back one cool evening after unwinding with some good old friends and met Ivy. Ivy was one of the younger best mentees of Suzy and also a good friend of both of us. She was an intelligent lady and a go-getter. Her whole life revolved around her work. I had met with her a couple of times before but there was something different about her that day. I helped her get some work done in my home office which was not unusual. I looked at her and she looked beautiful, I do not know what came over me when I kissed her on her lips in the office. After that, I thought she would punch me, push me, slap me or worse report me. Instead, she whispered 'what took you so long?' That was when we began an intensive affair.

I wasn't one to give excuses to my wife but I started to do so. I started to ignore my wife, blame my wife for every trivial thing and found everything she did wrong. I had issues with her and began arguments over silly little things, from her cooking to how she slept, her snoring, how fat she had become and even the noise she made when she ate. My wife's consistent prayer life became annoying to me now and her sweet morning praises now choked me. I complained about everything and looking back, I wonder how anyone could change as I did."

"Gradually, my Suzy got to find out about my affair with Ivy and it broke her heart. I remember her crying every day and sinking into a deep depression which led to a stroke. I came home one day after I had spent a few days with Ivy and met my wife on the bathroom floor. I thought she was dead and rushed her to the emergency ward where I requested the best doctors to help her recover. She made her full recovery after six gruelling months but she wasn't the same woman I had married. During those six months, Ivy had moved into my house, yes, the home my wife and I had built together. I got my wife a maid and a private home nurse and sent my wife to her hometown under the excuse she needed to recuperate. She cried, she begged and my daughters even begged along with their mother, but my stubborn and hardened heart would not listen to them. My pride, ego and the enjoyment I was having with Ivy were too much to sacrifice."

Out of anger, Maame shouted, "you are wicked and deserve everything you are going through even though I don't have a clue". Many people more particularly married women in the room started to murmur among themselves until Mrs Mona had to calm everyone and implored that they gave the man a chance to finish his story. She reminded them not to judge anyone prematurely.

When the atmosphere in the room calmed, he continued, "please let me finish, it has taken me two years to get to the place". As if in response, another man responded by telling him to keep on living with his guilt. The man broke down in tears and went to his knees as if talking to an unforeseen being. Mrs Mona beckoned him to pull himself together and go on.

After wiping his tears and getting himself together, he continued, "I used to visit her once every month but then reduced it to once every other month. Whenever I visited her, we would just stare at each other because there seemed to be nothing to talk about. The once most beautiful lady in my eyes just sat and stared at me without making any movements. It seemed that after over thirty years of marriage, there was nothing to talk about and so I stopped visiting altogether and went to enjoy my life with my young Ivy."

"I started to receive several messages from the townsfolk where my wife lived that she was in a bad condition. It was one such message that got me furious because it made me drive all the way there only to find her looking much better than I had expected or anticipated. It made me very furious because I thought I had been lied to just to get me to drive all the way there. I vented my anger on her. She began to cry, it seems that was all she did, cry. She begged me again, saying how sorry she was and asking us to get back together but my heart was hardened. As I was taking my leave, I decided I needed to end things with her if I was to solidify my life with Ivy. My wife looked pitiful, I hugged her for the last time and told her it was over. Yes, our marriage of over thirty years was called off with a hug. Susan knelt even in her condition and sobbed as I had never seen before. She repeatedly told me she would kill herself because she had nothing to live for. In my anger, I told her to kill herself because she was no longer useful to anyone. I left in anger. Now, I wish I could take those words back!"

I went back to the city and poured myself my celebratory favourite whiskey as I sat on the sofa with Ivy that evening. My cell phone rang and kept ringing. I was not in the mood to talk with any other person. I just wanted to enjoy my night of freedom with Ivy and my whiskey. I turned off my phone. The landline also started to ring and in my anger, I went to have it disconnected. I went to bed that night and made love to Ivy as I had never done before, I was free and that was what mattered to me at that moment. 'Tomorrow' I thought, 'I would see my lawyers to begin the divorce proceedings' I slept off.

In the morning, I reconnected the landline and before I could turn away, the phone rang. I picked up the receiver as I held a cup of sweetened tea in my hands.

"... Susan died yesterday an hour after you left. She got hold of a kitchen knife and slit her wrists. By the time the maid entered the house and managed to take her to the hospital, she was already dead and pronounced dead on arrival" the voice said at the other end of the line. "For a moment, I went numb, I dropped the cup of tea I was holding in my hand and collapsed. I couldn't breathe or scream, I could hear in a distance the other person on the line shouting 'hello, hello, are you there?' Before I lost consciousness, I saw my life play before my eyes. Ivy found me and rushed me to the hospital."

"After the solemn burial of my wife, my children did not want anything to do with me and I did not want anything to do with Ivy. I wished I could run away from myself. Alcohol became my friend and consoled me because all my friends, family and in-laws blamed me. No one took my side and they were right in doing so. There were times I contemplated suicide just to see my wife and ask for her forgiveness for my folly. If I couldn't apologise in this world, I should apologise in the next I thought. The guilt I carry around with me is eating me every day and I am truly grateful for this group. Little by little, I am learning to forgive myself."

"Harrison is my name" he concluded and left the stage walking like a huge weight had been lifted off his shoulders. There was not a single dry eye in the room when he was done with his story. What a day, what a story.

CHAPTER 7

Sharing the stories had been a good way to understand others and for a little while walk in their shoes. For months Maame had never missed a meeting and the results in her life were truly amazing. She had become a better person but she had one question that seemed unanswered. Today she would find out before the meeting ended.

As she walked into the meeting room, she was greeted by the chirpy Mrs. Mona and as usual, her husband who seemed to want to be at any other place but there. Maame pulled Mrs. Mona to the side "I am truly grateful for all you have done –" she began. "- I wouldn't know what I would have done was it not for this support group. May God bless you, dear." "Amen", Mrs. Mona replied. "Is there anything you want to talk about such that you got me into this corner to talk?" Mrs. Mona asked. "Well –" Maame began shyly" – I have always wanted to know your story. Surely there must have been a reason for you to organize such meetings to help people like me. What drove you to do this? Is it just a calling given to you or did something happen? My mother once told me the happiest people are those with the saddest stories. I am quite sure you have a hidden story and I am not one to pry but I have been curious about it for so long that I only wanted to know. Maybe your story would give me that final push I need to help others too." Maame spoke frankly. "If you don't wish to share it, that is fine as well." Mrs. Mona no longer had a smile on her face. Instead, there was a sadness about her. She replied softly "Today I would tell everyone my story. I think you all deserve to know" she winked and walked away.

Unlike what usually happened at the meetings, Mrs. Mona did not go round today to greet everybody in the room. This time she walked straight to the front and lifted her hand. "I have a story to share," she said. The bustle in the room stopped. What story could one of the happiest people anyone could ever meet have? But something was different about Mrs. Mona. She wasn't her bubbly self anymore, she seemed serious. Everyone took their seats and paid attention.

"I know some of you may have wondered what right I have to stand here and help you. A happy person like myself could possibly have no sad story. Well, like a friend just told me, the happiest people sometimes have the saddest story. My daughter is a suicide survivor." Everyone had their eyes wide open. Even this lovely woman went through this too? Maame thought. "Yes, I know it may come as a surprise to you. But she wasn't the perfect child and I did not have a perfect life. She got pregnant at fifteen and her father – " gesturing to her husband at the back who looked like he wanted to vanish from his spot "-had stopped talking to her". He stood up and walked to the front and said, "it's alright, you can share this." Rubbing a hand on her back, she mouthed a thank you before he walked off the stage to his usual spot. Everyone was frozen still.

"She wanted to take her life thinking she had disappointed us and would rather die than give birth. I started to see signs of depression in her mannerisms and sometimes the questions she asked me. I knew she was frustrated and I only thought it was hormonal changes associated with the pregnancy" she sniffed and took a tissue from her purse. "I did not take it to heart. One day I got back from work only to see my baby girl lying in a pool of her blood. She had slit her wrist and was bleeding profusely. She was unconscious from all the blood loss and cold to the touch. Before I could think twice I tore my dress and tied her wrists to stop the bleeding and carried my pregnant daughter to the car rushing her to the hospital. That day I gave more blood than I had ever thought I could. I told the nurses to take all my blood if that would save my daughter. I was informed that if I had brought her to the hospital three minutes later, she would have died. I stayed by her side and nursed her to health. I did not understand where it had all gone wrong."

"That experience broke us. It made us realise how much these kids go through and what parents suffer after their kids committed suicide. The thought of my girl not surviving was enough to traumatize me for about a year. I was put into therapy and when that seemed not to work group therapy was recommended. I joined a group like this one and started from there. The stories they shared, the support, and the way I could open up allowed me to heal faster. Today my daughter is alive and well and I have an energetic grandson. My life turned out better but I realized others did not have it as I did. I made a vow to help anyone like myself who may have been a suicide survivor, lost someone from suicide, or even had suicidal thoughts. That for me is my way of saving others," she concluded.

If a pin had fallen in the room, it would have been the loudest noise at that moment. Then someone clapped. It resounded and others joined slowly, soon it was a standing ovation for the woman who had helped them all.

Conclusion

It truly is a dark place to be when you go through life without a shoulder to lean on. When the frustrations of life become larger than the joy in this life, it may seem like it is not worth the fight. To the young ones reading this, don't do it. Don't take your own life because of a single mistake. Talk to somebody who can help you. Taking your life is a selfish act because you leave behind pain and sorrow that may take years to repair and in some cases may never get repaired. Parents who lose their children to suicide are never the same again. They love you regardless of how it may seem. No mother or father wants to bury your dead body over a matter that could be solved.

To parents who have lost their children to suicide, forgive yourself. You are not at fault for their death. You did not fail as a parent and don't let anyone tell you any less. Move on, learn to smile again. Speak to a counselor, seek help and get better. Help someone else so they don't have to go through what you are going through.

To everyone else who picked up this book, mental health issues are real. Depression is on the rise and people need someone to talk to. You may have noticed a friend who shows signs of depression or even talks of taking their life as a joke. Be there for them so they do not do it. Be the shoulder someone can lean on with as little as lending a listening ear. Don't think a happy person does not have an issue. There are cases of people who seemed happy one moment and took their lives the next moment.

Suicide destroys not just the life that was taken but also the lives of the people left behind. Be strong and brave. I wish you the best in life!

www.ingramcontent.com/pod-product-compliance
Lightning Source LLC
LaVergne TN
LVHW010459160826
845677LV00012B/2554

* 9 7 9 8 8 4 5 9 7 0 4 6 6 *